Down by the Station

BY WILL HILLENBRAND

Voyager Books · Harcourt, Inc.

SAN DIEGO   NEW YORK   LONDON

Requests for permission to make copies of any part of the work should be submitted online at www.harcourt.com/contact or mailed to the following address:
Permissions Department,
Houghton Mifflin Harcourt Publishing Company,
6277 Sea Harbor Drive, Orlando, Florida 32887-6777.

www.HarcourtBooks.com

First Voyager Books edition 2002
Voyager Books is a trademark of Harcourt, Inc., registered in the United States of America and/or other jurisdictions.

The Library of Congress has cataloged the hardcover edition as follows:
Hillenbrand, Will.
Down by the station/by Will Hillenbrand.
p.   cm.
Summary: In this version of a familiar song, baby animals ride to the children's zoo on the zoo train.
1. Children's songs—Texts.   [1. Zoo animals—Songs and music.   2. Animals—Infancy—Songs and music.   3. Songs.]
I. Title.
PZ8.3.H553Do   1999
782.42—dc21
[E]   98-41770
ISBN 978-0-15-201804-7
ISBN 978-0-15-216790-5 pb

TWP   16 15 14 13 12 11 10
4500276572

Printed in Singapore

The illustrations in this book were created in mixed media on vellum, painted on both sides.
The display type was set in Belwe Bold Condensed.
The text type was set in Worcester Round Bold.
Color separations by Bright Arts Ltd., Hong Kong
Printed in Singapore by Tien Wah Press Pte Ltd
Production supervision by Sandra Grebenar and Wendi Taylor
Designed by Kaelin Chappell and Will Hillenbrand

To Liz; Charlie;
my wife, Jane;
and my son, Ian

Down by the station
early in the morning.

See the little puffer-bellies
all in a row.

See the engine driver
pull his little lever. . . .

Puff, puff,
Toot, toot,
Off we go!

Down by the elephants
early in the morning.
See the little calf
waiting to go.
See the engine driver
pull his little lever. . . .

Puff, puff,
Toot, toot,
Thrump, thrump,
Off we go!

Down by the flamingos
early in the morning.
See the little chick
waiting to go.
See the engine driver
pull his little lever. . . .

Puff, puff,
Toot, toot,
Thrump, thrump,
Peep, peep,
Off we go!

Down by the pandas
early in the morning.
See the little cub
waiting to go.
See the engine driver
pull his little lever. . . .

Puff, puff,
Toot, toot,
Thrump, thrump,
Peep, peep,
Grump, grump,
Off we go!

Down by the tigers
early in the morning.
See the little cub
waiting to go.
See the engine driver
pull his little lever. . . .

Puff, puff,
Toot, toot,
Thrump, thrump,
Peep, peep,
Grump, grump,
Mew, mew,
Off we go!

Seal Island

Down by the seals
early in the morning.
See the little pup
waiting to go.
See the engine driver
pull his little lever. . . .

Puff, puff,
Toot, toot,
Thrump, thrump,
Peep, peep,
Grump, grump,
Mew, mew,
Flip, flop . . .

DANGER

Down by the kangaroos
early in the morning.
See the little joey
waiting to go.

See the engine driver
pull his little lever....

Puff, puff,
Toot, toot,
Thrump, thrump,
Peep, peep,
Grump, grump,
Mew, mew,
Flip, flop,
Bump, bump,
Off we go!

Down by the children's zoo
early in the morning.
See the baby animals
exit in a row.
See the engine driver
pull his little lever. . . .

Puff, puff,
Toot, toot . . .

Off we go!

Down by the Station